TITCH
AND
DAISY

Pat Hutchins

TITCH AND

RED FOX

DAISY

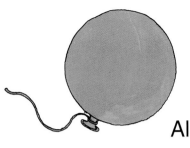

Also by Pat Hutchins

Titch
Tidy Titch
You'll Soon Grow Into Them, Titch
We're Going On a Picnic!
Rosie's Walk
The Shrinking Mouse
Don't Forget the Bacon
Ten Red Apples

TITCH AND DAISY
A Red Fox Book: 0 09 971801 4

First published in Great Britain by Julia MacRae,
an imprint of Random House Children's Books

Julia MacRae edition published 1996
Red Fox edition 1997; this edition 2002

3 5 7 9 10 8 6 4 2

First published by Greenwillow Books, New York, USA, 1996

Red Fox Books are published by Random House Children's Books,
61-63 Uxbridge Road, London W5 5SA,
a division of The Random House Group, Ltd,
in Australia by Random House Australia (Pty) Ltd,
20 Alfred Street, Milsons Point, Sydney, NSW 2061, Australia,
in New Zealand by Random House New Zealand Ltd,
18 Poland Road, Glenfield, Auckland 10, New Zealand,
and in South Africa by Random House (Pty) Ltd,
Endulini, 5A Jubilee Road, Parktown 2193, South Africa

THE RANDOM HOUSE GROUP Limited Reg. No. 954009
www.kidsatrandomhouse.co.uk

A CIP catalogue record for this book is available from the British Library.

Printed in Singapore

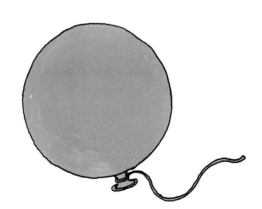

For Barbara and Henning
to read to their grandchildren

Titch didn't want to go
to the party.
"You'll make new friends,"
said Mother, "and Daisy
will be there."

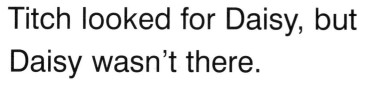

Titch looked for Daisy, but
Daisy wasn't there.
"Hello," said the other children.
"Come and play with us!"
But Titch didn't want to play
if Daisy wasn't there.

He hid behind the door and watched them playing all his favourite games.
He wished Daisy were there.

"Come and dance with us!"
said the other children.
But Titch didn't want to dance
if Daisy wasn't there.

So he crept behind the sofa
and watched them dancing
all his favourite dances.
He wished Daisy were there.

"Come and sing with us!" said
the other children.
But Titch didn't want to sing
if Daisy wasn't there.

So he peeped out of the cupboard and listened to them singing all his favourite songs. He wished Daisy were there.

"Come and eat with us!" said
the other children.
But Titch didn't want to eat
if Daisy wasn't there.

He crawled under the table,
which was covered with all his
favourite things to eat.
He wished Daisy were there.

And she was.

"I hid under the table when I couldn't find you," said Daisy. "I kept wishing you were here."

"PLEASE come and eat with us,"
said the other children.
And Titch and Daisy did.

They ate all their favourite food.

And they danced,
and sang
all their favourite songs,

and played all their
favourite games,

and made lots of new friends.